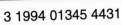

Shrinking
Sam

To Ali and Jules (who used to think he would
fall down the drain!) — M. L.

Barefoot Books
2067 Massachusetts Ave
Cambridge, MA 02140

Graphic design by Judy Linard, London
Color separation by Grafiscan, Verona
Printed and bound in China by PrintPlus Ltd

This book was typeset in Zemke Hand ITC
The illustrations were prepared in acrylics and collage

Library of Congress Cataloging-in-Publication Data

Latimer, Miriam.
  Shrinking Sam / Miriam Latimer.
    p. cm.
  Summary: When no one pays attention to him at home or at school,
Sam feels himself shrinking away to nothing, but a little advice from a
small friend and some affection from his family soon restore him to his
normal height.
  ISBN-13: 978-1-84686-038-6 (hardcover : alk. paper)
  [1. Size--Fiction. 2. Family life--Fiction.] I. Title.

PZ7.L369625Shr 2007
[E]--dc22
                                          2006021585

135798642

Shrinking
Sam

Written and illustrated by
Miriam Latimer

Barefoot Books
Celebrating Art and Story

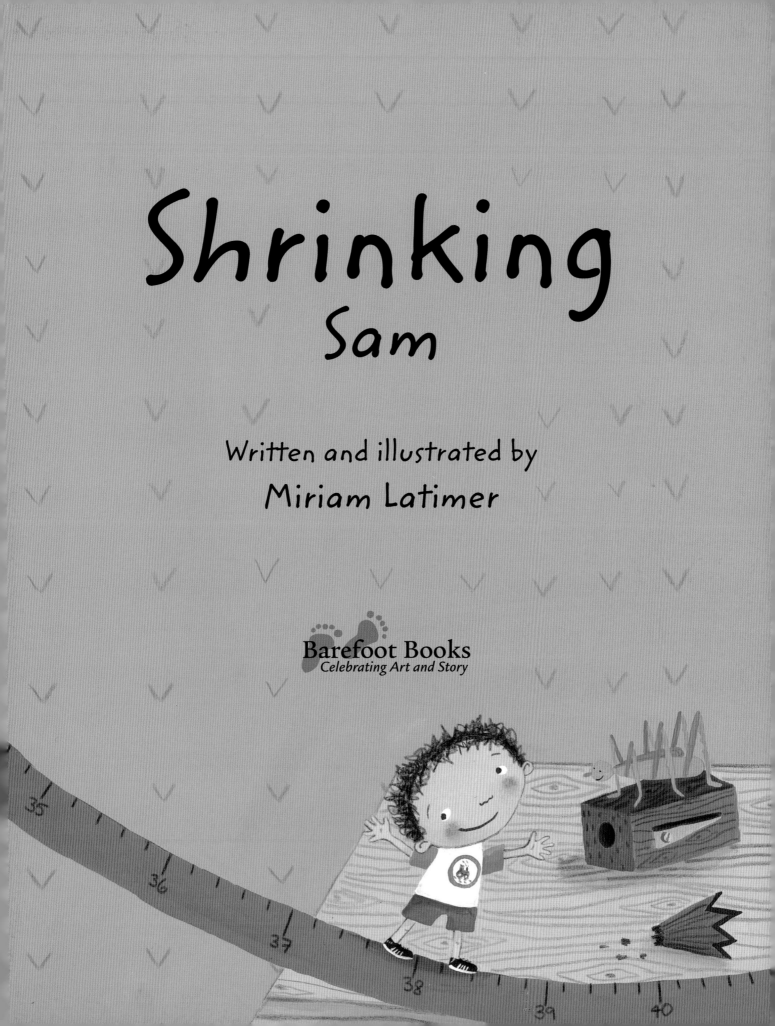

"Mom, I think I'm shrinking," said Sam. "I couldn't reach my breakfast this morning, and now I can't reach my coat, and I'm DEFINITELY not as tall as yesterday."

"Mmm, lovely, honey," said Mom. "Now get ready for school, or you'll miss the bus again."

By the time Sam had gotten to school,
he was sure he had shrunk even more.
"Where's your reading book, Sam?"
asked Mrs. Barratt.
"Mrs. Barratt, I've shrunk so small,
my pencil is the size of a crocodile,
and I think it's trying to
eat me."

Mrs. Barratt sent Sam home with a note.
"Sam is getting too big for his boots.
NO MORE NONSENSE," she wrote.

At dinnertime, the peas on Sam's plate were so BIG, just one of them filled his whole tummy.
"Dad, I'm definitely shrinking. I'm as small as a tomato. Pete, I'm knee-high to a grasshopper!"

"Mom, Sam's throwing peas at me again!" Pete said.
"Go and take your bath, Sam, and leave your brother alone," said Mom.

Sam slid down to the floor and
climbed into the flowerpot.
Kimba the dog bounded over.
He seemed like a giant.

"Kimba, I'm shrinking.
What am I going to do?
Oh no, Kimba, don't..."

"Ahh, Ahhhhh, Ahhhhhhh...

. . . Choooo!"
Kimba gave an enormous sneeze, and Sam,
who was now as light as a feather, floated
all the way up to the top of the stairs.

But the bath was far too big for Sam.
So he climbed up the side of a towel
and played in the sink.
"Why doesn't anyone listen
to me?" he shouted.

As Sam washed, the water began to swirl around. Faster and faster it swirled, and as it swirled it dropped lower and lower. The plug had come out!

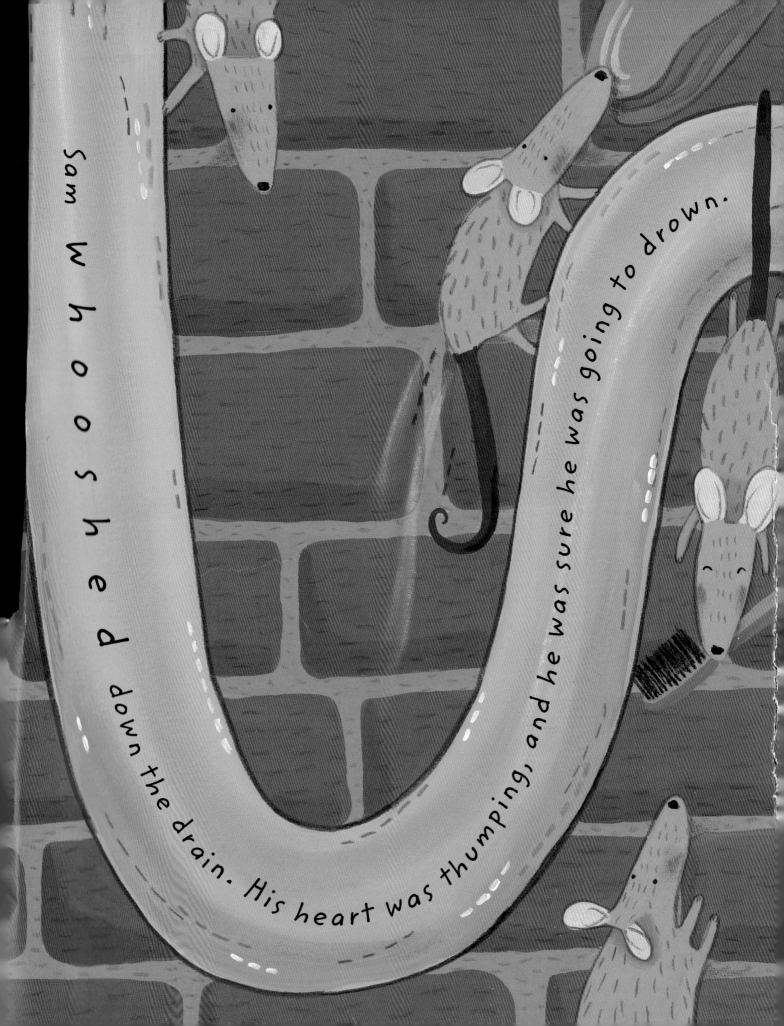

Sam whooshed down the drain. His heart was thumping, and he was sure he was going to drown.

"Oh no!" Sam cried, as he felt himself being sucked down the drain.

"HELP!"

As the drain grew darker and colder, he began to shiver.
"I—i—is anyone there?" he stuttered.
He was shivering all over and his teeth were chattering.
"I—i—is anyone there?" his voice echoed back. Sam began to cry.

"Quick! Grab hold of this!" came a small voice, and Sam felt himself being pulled up on to a floating sponge.

"Who are you?" he asked, staring at the small girl on top of the sponge.

"I'm Izzy," she replied cheerfully.
"This happens to me all the time.
I shrink every time my family
ignores me. Today, I shrank so
much that I fell down the toilet.
Why are you so small?"

"The same thing happened to me, but I fell down the sink," explained Sam, staring at her. As the two children shared their stories, they started to grow a little and as they listened to each other, they grew a little more.

"Hooray, I'm starting to grow!" cried Sam.
"And so are you!"
Izzy just smiled. "Come on," she said.
"We need to start paddling."

"I can see a light ahead,"
called Izzy. "I think it's your
home."
"What about you?" asked Sam.
"Don't worry. The next stop's
my house."

"Bye, Izzy, and thank you." Sam leapt off the sponge and into the light. He landed with a thump in a pile of damp clothes.

"Those are my pajamas, and that's Amy's T-shirt . . . I know where I am. I'm inside the washing machine! But how am I going to get out?"

"Woof!" barked Kimba from outside, and he bounded over, wagging his tail. He opened the door with his paw, and gave Sam a BIG lick. Sam felt himself grow a little bit bigger.

"Sam!" gurgled his baby sister.
"Wow, you've learned to say my name!"

Amy blew him a kiss through the air, and Sam felt himself grow even bigger.

"Hello, Sam!" said Dad.
"Have you taken your
bath?" asked Mom.
"We wondered what
you were up to.
We thought you
might have
fallen down the
drain!"

Sam grinned as Mom
and Dad gave him
a BIG LONG hug . . .

. . . and he felt himself grow even bigger than before!
"I'm starving!" he said. "Is there anything to eat?"

Barefoot Books
Celebrating Art and Story

At Barefoot Books, we celebrate art and story that opens
the hearts and minds of children from all walks of life, inspiring
them to read deeper, search further, and explore their own creative gifts.
Taking our inspiration from many different cultures, we focus on themes that
encourage independence of spirit, enthusiasm for learning, and sharing of
the world's diversity. Interactive, playful and beautiful, our products
combine the best of the present with the best of the past to
educate our children as the caretakers of tomorrow.

Live Barefoot!
Join us at www.barefootbooks.com

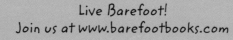